Bad Boys

Get Henpecked!

by Margie Palatini ◆ illustrated by Henry Cole

KATHERINE TEGEN BOOKS
An Imprint of HarperCollinsPublishers

Also by Margie Palatini and Henry Cole

Bad Boys

Bad Boys Get Cookie!

Bad Boys Get Henpecked!
Text copyright © 2009 by Margie Palatini
Illustrations copyright © 2009 by Henry Cole
Manufactured in China.

Library of Congress Cataloging-in-Publication Data
Palatini, Margie.
    Bad boys get henpecked! / by Margie Palatini ; illustrated by Henry Cole. — 1st ed.
        p.   cm.
    Summary: Bad boy wolves Willy and Wally try to get a chicken dinner by disguising
themselves as the Handy-Dandy Lupino Brothers and going to work for a hen in need of
household help.
    ISBN 978-0-06-074433-5 (trade bdg.) — ISBN 978-0-06-074434-2 (lib. bdg.)
    [1. Wolves—Fiction.   2. Chickens—Fiction.   3. Humorous stories.]   I. Cole, Henry, date
ill.   II. Title.
PZ7.P1755Bd   2009   2008011771
[E]—dc22   CIP
                                                                        AC

Typography by Jeanne L. Hogle
09 10 11 12 13 LEO 10 9 8 7 6 5 4 3
❖
First Edition

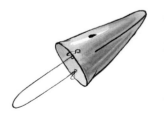

To my Handy-Dandy Mr. Lupino
—M.P.

To Quinn
—Hen

Those bad boys, Willy and Wally Wolf, were hungry. Belly-babbling, tummy-talking, gut-grumbling hungry.

And what better to wolf down than a delicious, delectable, finger-lickin'-good . . . Chicken Dinner—with leftover sandwiches for the week! "Oh yeah, we're bad, bad, really, really bad," snickered the two with a slobber and a slurp as they eyed the old henhouse.

Of course, running off with the lovely, fat feathered fowl was not going to be easy. Not one bit. Getting into the coop and gaining the trust of the lady of the house was going to take finesse. Wile. One big sneaky trick.

Willy looked at Wally. Wally looked at Willy. The two giggled. Brain ditto!

What that little woman needed was some help around the house.

And who better for the job than—the Handy-Dandy Lupino Brothers!

"This plan is perfecto!" chuckled Willy.

"We'll clean up and take-out," chortled Wally.

"How devious. How deceitful. How perfectly delightful!"
Yes. Those boys were bad. Bad. Really, really bad.

"Good day, madam," greeted Willy as Mrs. Hen opened the door. "Are you tired? Run-down? Pooped? Is your roof leaking? Paint peeling? Need the lawn mowed? A lightbulb changed? Then the Handy-Dandy Lupino Brothers are at your service!"

"Good gracious," clucked the hen. "You gentlemen are just what I need. That old rooster of mine has flown the coop and I could use some help around the house. But all I can afford to pay is mere chicken feed."

Willy winked at Wally. Wally winked at Willy.

"*Chicken feed?*" said Willy with a sly smile. "Madam, we *love* getting paid in chicken feed!"

"Absolutely adore it!" agreed Wally with a bit of a drool. "We work for *cheep*."

The hen threw off her apron. "When can you start?"

The bad boys grinned from ear to ear. "Immediately!" they both answered.

But before the boys could reach into their pockets for napkins, Mrs. Hen handed them two aprons, a bucket, and a mop.

Willy looked at Wally. "Bucket?"

Wally looked at Willy. "Mop?"

They both looked at each other. "Aprons?"

"Here's a list of what to do. I'll be back before supper," Mrs. Hen called over her shoulder. "Ta-ta! So long! Good luck!"

The boys watched their chicken dinner fly out the door.

They gazed down at the list. . . . It was a very long list.

Sweep the porch. Mop the kitchen. Scrub the bathroom.
Vacuum the rugs. Dust the tables. Polish the silverware.
Wash the clothes. Hang the clothes. Iron the clothes. Watch
the chickies. Bathe the chickies. Feather the nest. Sit on the nest.

And—take out the garbage!

"Housework!"

This wasn't exactly what they had planned.

"*Peep! Peep! Peep! Peep! Peep! Peep! Peep!*" The chickies pecked, poked, and pulled at Willy. Then pecked, poked, and pulled at Wally.

Willy groaned. "*I'll* start the laundry. *You* take care of the chickies—and no snacking before dinner!"

So Wally watched. Watched.
Watched.

While Willy washed. Washed. Washed.
And swept. Mopped. Dusted. Polished.
Vacuumed. Scoured. Scrubbed.

And Wally watched.
Watched. Watched.

"I'm exhausted," huffed Willy.

"You, dear chum? I'm about to faint!" puffed Wally. "All that peeping has given me a splitting headache! I must lie down!"

Brain ditto!

"Last one to the nest is a rotten egg!" they both said, heading for the hay.

"Feels a little lumpy," said Willy, trying to get comfy.

"I must say, I feel a tad silly as well," said Wally, trying to find a soft spot.

They both giggled. "What the hey!"

The two yawned, closed their eyes, and began snoozing away in a snoring duet.

The little chickies were left to amuse themselves.
And they did. Oh my, they did.

"P'awk! P'awk! P'awk!"

"Mr. Lupino! Mr. Lupino!" cried Mrs. Hen as she walked through the door. "What exactly has been going on here?"

"I do believe we are being dismissed, dear boy."

"Canned. Ousted.
Fired!" said Mrs. Hen.

"Brain ditto! We are most definitely out of here!"

"I do believe I have lost my taste for chicken," said Willy.

"Couldn't agree more, dear pal," said Wally. "Besides . . . I'm just too tired to cook tonight."

Those henpecked bad boys ate their peanut butter and jelly sandwiches.

They wanted to say it was a bad, bad, really, really bad day.

But they could not.

The peanut butter was stuck to the roofs of their mouths.